THE HAUNTED BOOKSHELF

he telling or reading of ghost stories during long, dark, and cold Christmas nights is a yuletide ritual dating back to at least the eighteenth century, and was once as much a part of Christmas tradition as decorating fir trees, feasting on goose, and the singing of carols. During the Victorian era many magazines printed ghost stories specifically for the Christmas season. These "winter tales" didn't necessarily explore Christmas themes. Rather, they were offered as an eerie pleasure to be enjoyed on Christmas Eve with the family, adding a supernatural shiver to the seasonal chill.

The tradition remained strong in the British Isles (and her colonies) throughout much of the twentieth century, though in recent years it has been on the wane. Certainly, few people in Canada or the United States seem to know about it any longer. This series of small books seeks to rectify this, to revive a charming custom for the long, dark nights we all know so well here at Christmastime.

THE HAUNTED BOOKSHELF

THE HAUNTED BOOKSHELF

THE DEAD
AND THE COUNTESS

THE DEAD AND THE COUNTESS

COUNTESS

GERTRUDE ATHERTON

A GHOST STORY FOR CHRISTMAS

DESIGNED & DECORATED BY SETH

BIBLIOASIS

I T WAS AN OLD CEMETERY, and they had been long dead. Those who died nowadays were put in the new burying-place on the hill, close to the Bois d'Amour and within sound of the bells that called the living to mass. But the little church where the mass was celebrated stood faithfully beside the older dead; a new church, indeed, had not been built in that forgotten corner of Finisterre for centuries, not since the calvary on its pile of stones had been raised in the tiny square, surrounded then, as now, perhaps, by grey naked cottages; not since the castle with its round tower, down on the river, had been erected for the Counts of Croisac. But the stone walls enclosing that ancient cemetery had been kept in good repair, and there were no weeds within, nor toppling headstones. It looked cold and grey and desolate, like all the cemeteries of Brittany, but it was made hideous neither by tawdry gewgaws nor the license of time.

And sometimes it was close to a picture of beauty. When the village celebrated its yearly *pardon*, a great procession came out of the church—priests in glittering robes, young men in their gala costume of black and silver, holding flashing standards aloft, and many maidens in flapping white head-dress and collar, black frocks and aprons flaunting with ribbons and lace. They marched, chanting, down the road beside the wall of the cemetery, where lay the generations that in their day had held the banners and chanted the service of the *pardon*. For the dead were peasants and priests—the Croisacs had their burying-place in a hollow of the hills behind the castle—old men and women who had wept and died for the fishermen that had gone to the *grande pêche* and returned no more, and now and again a child, slept there. Those who walked past the dead at the *pardon*, or after the marriage ceremony, or took part in any one of the minor religious festivals with which the Catholic village enlivens its existence—all, young and old, looked grave and sad. For the women from childhood know that their lot is to wait and dread and weep, and the men that the ocean is treacherous and cruel, but that bread can be wrung from no other master. Therefore the living have little sympathy for the dead who have laid down their crushing burden; and the dead under their stones slumber contentedly enough. There is no envy among them for the young who wander at evening and pledge their troth in the Bois d'Amour, only pity for the groups of women who wash their linen in the creek that flows to the river. They look like pictures in the green quiet book of nature, these women, in their glistening white head-gear and deep collars; but the dead know better than to envy them, and the women—and the lovers—know better than to pity the dead.

The dead lay at rest in their boxes and thanked God they were quiet and had found everlasting peace.

And one day even this, for which they had patiently endured life, was taken from them.

The village was picturesque and there was none quite like it, even in Finisterre. Artists discovered it and made it famous. After the artists followed the tourists, and the old creaking *diligence* became an absurdity. Brittany was the fashion for three months of the year, and wherever there is fashion there is at least one railway. The one built to satisfy the thousands who wished to visit the wild, sad beauties of the west of France was laid along the road beside the little cemetery of this tale.

It takes a long while to awaken the dead. These heard neither the voluble working-men nor even the first snort of the engine. And, of course, they neither heard nor knew of the pleadings of the old priest that the line should be laid elsewhere. One night he came out into the old cemetery and sat on a grave and wept. For he loved his dead and felt it to be a tragic pity that the greed of money, and the fever of travel, and the petty ambitions of men whose place was in the great cities where such ambitions were born, should shatter forever the holy calm of those who had suffered so much on earth. He had known many of them in life, for he was very old; and although he believed, like all good Catholics, in heaven and purgatory and hell, yet he always saw his friends as he had buried them, peacefully asleep in their coffins, the souls lying with folded hands like the bodies that held them, patiently awaiting the final call. He would never have told you, this good old priest, that he believed heaven to be a great echoing palace in which God and the archangels dwelt alone waiting for that great day when the elected dead should rise and enter the Presence together, for he was a simple old man who had read and thought little; but he had a zigzag of fancy in his humble mind, and he saw his friends and his ancestors' friends as I have related to you, soul and body in the deep undreaming sleep of death, but sleep, not a rotted body deserted by its affrighted mate; and to all who sleep there comes, sooner or later, the time of awakening.

He knew that they had slept through the wild storms that rage on the coast of Finisterre, when ships are flung on the rocks and trees crash down in the Bois d'Amour. He knew that the soft, slow chantings of the *pardon* never struck a chord in those frozen memories, meagre and monotonous as their store had been; nor the bagpipes down in the open village hall—a mere roof on poles—when the bride and her friends danced for three days without a smile on their sad brown faces.

All this the dead had known in life and it could not disturb nor interest them now. But that hideous intruder from modern civilization, a train of cars with a screeching engine, that would shake the earth which held them and rend the peaceful air with such discordant sounds that neither dead nor living could sleep! His life had been one long unbroken sacrifice, and he sought in vain to imagine one greater, which he would cheerfully assume could this disaster be spared his dead.

But the railway was built, and the first night the train went screaming by, shaking the earth and rattling the windows of the church, he went out and sprinkled every grave with holy water.

And thereafter, twice a day, at dawn and at night, as the train tore a noisy tunnel in the quiet air, like the plebeian upstart it was, he sprinkled every grave, rising sometimes from a bed of pain, at other times defying wind and rain and hail. And for a while he believed that his holy device had deepened the sleep of his dead, locked them beyond the power of man to awake. But one night he heard them muttering.

It was late. There were but a few stars on a black sky. Not a breath of wind came over the lonely plains beyond, or from the sea. There would be no wrecks tonight, and all the world seemed at peace. The lights were out in the village. One burned in the tower of Croisac, where the young wife of the count lay ill. The priest had been with her when the train thundered by, and she had whispered to him:

"Would that I were on it! Oh, this lonely, lonely land! This cold echoing château, with no one to speak to day after day! If it kills me, *mon père*, make him lay me in the cemetery by the road, that twice a day I may hear the train go by—the train that goes to Paris! If they put me down there over the hill, I will shriek in my coffin every night."

The priest had ministered as best he could to the ailing soul of the young noble-woman, with whose like he seldom dealt, and hastened back to his dead. He mused, as he toiled along the dark road with rheumatic legs, on the fact that the woman should have the same fancy as himself.

"If she is really sincere, poor young thing," he thought aloud, "I will forbear to sprinkle holy water on her grave. For those who suffer while alive should have all they desire after death, and I am afraid the count neglects her. But I pray God that my dead have not heard that monster tonight." And he tucked his gown under his arm and hurriedly told his rosary.

But when he went about among the graves with the holy water he heard the dead muttering.

"Jean-Marie," said a voice, fumbling among its unused tones for forgotten notes, "art thou ready? Surely that is the last call."

"Nay, nay," rumbled another voice, "that is not the sound of a trumpet, François. That will be sudden and loud and sharp, like the great blasts of the north when they come plunging over the sea from out the awful gorges of Iceland. Dost thou remember them, François? Thank the good God they spared us to die in our beds with our grandchildren about us and only the little wind sighing in the Bois d'Amour. Ah, the poor comrades that died in their manhood, that went to the *grande pêche* once too often! Dost thou remember when the great wave curled round Ignace like his poor wife's arms, and we saw him no more? We clasped each other's hands, for we believed that we should follow, but we lived and went again and again to the *grande pêche*, and died in our beds. *Grâce à Dieu!*"

"Why dost thou think of that now—here in the grave where it matters not, even to the living?"

"I know not; but it was of that night when Ignace went down that I thought as the living breath went out of me. Of what didst thou think as thou layest dying?"

"Of the money I owed to Dominique and could not pay. I sought to ask my son to pay it, but death had come suddenly and I could not speak. God knows how they treat my name today in the village of St. Hilaire."

"Thou art forgotten," murmured another voice. "I died forty years after thee and men

remember not so long in Finisterre. But thy son was my friend and I remember that he paid the money."

"And my son, what of him? Is he, too, here?"

"Nay; he lies deep in the northern sea. It was his second voyage, and he had returned with a purse for the young wife, the first time. But he returned no more, and she washed in the river for the dames of Croisac, and by-and-by she died. I would have married her, but she said it was enough to lose one husband. I married another, and she grew ten years in every three that I went to the *grande pêche*. Alas for Brittany, she has no youth!"

"And thou? Wert thou an old man when thou camest here?"

"Sixty. My wife came first, like many wives. She lies here. Jeanne!"

"Is't thy voice, my husband? Not the Lord Jesus Christ's? What miracle is this? I thought that terrible sound was the trump of doom."

"It could not be, old Jeanne, for we are still

in our graves. When the trump sounds we shall have wings and robes of light, and fly straight up to heaven. Hast thou slept well?"

"Ay! But why are we awakened? Is it time for purgatory? Or have we been there?"

"The good God knows. I remember nothing. Art frightened? Would that I could hold thy hand, as when thou didst slip from life into that long sleep thou didst fear, yet welcome."

"I am frightened, my husband. But it is sweet to hear thy voice, hoarse and hollow as it is from the mould of the grave. Thank the good God thou didst bury me with the rosary in my hands," and she began telling the beads rapidly.

"If God is good," cried François, harshly, and his voice came plainly to the priest's ears, as if the lid of the coffin had rotted, "why are we awakened before our time? What foul fiend was it that thundered and screamed through the frozen avenues of my brain?

Has God, perchance, been vanquished and does the Evil One reign in His stead?"

"Tut, tut! Thou blasphemest! God reigns, now and always. It is but a punishment He has laid upon us for the sins of earth."

"Truly, we were punished enough before we descended to the peace of this narrow house. Ah, but it is dark and cold! Shall we lie like this for an eternity, perhaps? On earth we longed for death, but feared the grave. I would that I were alive again, poor and old and alone and in pain. It were better than this. Curse the foul fiend that woke us!"

"Curse not, my son," said a soft voice, and the priest stood up and uncovered and crossed himself, for it was the voice of his aged predecessor. "I cannot tell thee what this is that has rudely shaken us in our graves and freed our spirits of their blessed thraldom, and I like not the consciousness of this narrow house, this load of earth on my tired heart. But it is right, it must be right, or it would not be at all—ah, me!"

For a baby cried softly, hopelessly, and from a grave beyond came a mother's anguished attempt to still it.

"Ah, the good God!" she cried. "I, too, thought it was the great call, and that in a moment I should rise and find my child and go to my Ignace, my Ignace whose bones lie white on the floor of the sea. Will he find them, my father, when the dead shall rise again? To lie here and doubt!—that were worse than life."

"Yes, yes," said the priest; "all will be well, my daughter."

"But all is not well, my father, for my baby cries and is alone in a little box in the ground. If I could claw my way to her with my hands—but my old mother lies between us."

"Tell your beads!" commanded the priest, sternly—"tell your beads, all of you. All ye that have not your beads, say the 'Hail Mary!' one hundred times."

Immediately a rapid, monotonous muttering arose from every lonely chamber of that desecrated ground. All obeyed but the baby, who still moaned with the hopeless grief of deserted children. The living priest knew that they would talk no more that night, and went into the church to pray till dawn. He was sick with horror and terror, but not for himself. When the sky was pink and the air full of the sweet scents of morning, and a piercing scream tore a rent in the early silences, he hastened out and sprinkled his graves with a double allowance of holy water. The train rattled by with two short derisive shrieks, and before the earth had ceased to tremble the priest laid his ear to the ground. Alas, they were still awake!

"The fiend is on the wing again," said Jean-Marie, "but as he passed I felt as if the finger of God touched my brow. It can do us no harm."

"I, too, felt that heavenly caress!" exclaimed

the old priest. "And I!" "And I!" "And I!" came from every grave but the baby's.

The priest of earth, deeply thankful that his simple device had comforted them, went rapidly down the road to the castle. He forgot that he had not broken his fast nor slept. The count was one of the directors of the railroad, and to him he would make a final appeal.

It was early, but no one slept at Croisac. The young countess was dead. A great bishop had arrived in the night and administered extreme unction. The priest hopefully asked if he might venture into the presence of the bishop. After a long wait in the kitchen, he was told that he could speak with *Monsieur l'Évêque*. He followed the servant up the wide spiral stair of the tower, and from its twenty-eighth step entered a room hung with purple cloth stamped with golden fleurs-de-lis. The bishop lay six feet above the floor on one of the splendid carved cabinet beds that are built against the walls

in Brittany. Heavy curtains shaded his cold white face. The priest, who was small and bowed, felt immeasurably below that august presence, and sought for words.

"What is it, my son?" asked the bishop, in his cold weary voice. "Is the matter so pressing? I am very tired."

Brokenly, nervously, the priest told his story, and as he strove to convey the tragedy of the tormented dead he not only felt the poverty of his expression—for he was little used to narrative—but the torturing thought assailed him that what he said sounded wild and unnatural, real as it was to him. But he was not prepared for its effect on the bishop. He was standing in the middle of the room, whose gloom was softened and gilded by the waxen lights of a huge candelabra; his eyes, which had wandered unseeingly from one massive piece of carved furniture to another, suddenly lit on the bed, and he stopped abruptly, his tongue rolling out. The bishop was sitting up, livid with wrath.

"And this was thy matter of life and death, thou prating madman!" he thundered. "For this string of foolish lies I am kept from my rest, as if I were another old lunatic like thyself! Thou art not fit to be a priest and have the care of souls. Tomorrow—"

But the priest had fled, wringing his hands.

As he stumbled down the winding stair he ran straight into the arms of the count. Monsieur de Croisac had just closed a door behind him. He opened it, and, leading the priest into the room, pointed to his dead countess, who lay high up against the wall, her hands clasped, unmindful forevermore of the six feet of carved cupids and lilies that upheld her. On high pedestals at head and foot of her magnificent couch the pale flames rose from tarnished golden candlesticks. The blue hangings of the room, with their white fleurs-de-lis, were faded, like the rugs on the old dim floor; for the splendor of the Croisacs had departed with the Bourbons. The count lived in the old château because he must; but he reflected bitterly tonight that if he had made the mistake of bringing a young girl to it, there were several things he might have done to save her from despair and death.

"Pray for her," he said to the priest. "And you will bury her in the old cemetery. It was her last request."

He went out, and the priest sank on his knees and mumbled his prayers for the dead. But his eyes wandered to the high narrow windows through which the countess had stared for hours and days, stared at the fishermen sailing north for the *grande pêche*, followed along the shore of the river by wives and mothers, until their boats were caught in the great waves of the ocean beyond; often at naught more animate than the dark flood, the wooded banks, the ruins, the rain driving like needles through the water. The priest had eaten nothing since his meagre breakfast at twelve the day before, and his imagination was active. He wondered if the soul up there rejoiced in the death of the beautiful restless body, the passionate brooding mind. He could not see her face from where he knelt, only the waxen hands clasping a crucifix. He wondered if the face were peaceful in death, or peevish and angry as when he had seen it last. If the great change had smoothed and sealed it, then perhaps the soul would sink deep under the dark waters, grateful for oblivion, and that cursed train could not awaken it for years to come. Curiosity succeeded wonder. He cut his prayers short, got to his weary swollen feet and pushed a chair to the bed. He mounted it and his face was close to the dead woman's. Alas! it was not peaceful. It was stamped with the tragedy of a bitter renunciation. After all, she had been young, and at the last had died unwillingly.

There was still a fierce tenseness about the nostrils, and her upper lip was curled as if her last word had been an imprecation. But she was very beautiful, despite the emaciation of her features. Her black hair nearly covered the bed, and her lashes looked too heavy for the sunken cheeks.

"*Pauvre petite!*" thought the priest. "No, she will not rest, nor would she wish to. I will not sprinkle holy water on her grave. It is wondrous that monster can give comfort to anyone, but if he can, so be it."

He went into the little oratory adjoining the bedroom and prayed more fervently. But when the watchers came an hour later they found him in a stupor, huddled at the foot of the altar.

When he awoke he was in his own bed in his little house beside the church. But it was four days before they would let him rise to go about his duties, and by that time the countess was in her grave.

The old housekeeper left him to take care of himself. He waited eagerly for the night. It was raining thinly, a grey quiet rain that blurred the landscape and soaked the ground in the Bois d'Amour. It was wet about the graves, too; but the priest had given little heed to the elements in his long life of crucified self, and as he heard the remote echo of the evening train he hastened out with his holy water and had sprinkled every grave but one when the train sped by.

Then he knelt and listened eagerly. It was five days since he had knelt there last. Perhaps they had sunk again to rest. In a moment he wrung his hands and raised them to heaven. All the earth beneath him was filled with lamentation. They wailed for mercy, for peace, for rest; they cursed the foul fiend who had shattered the locks of death; and among the voices of men and children the priest distinguished the quavering notes of his aged predecessor; not cursing, but praying with bitter entreaty. The baby was screaming with the accents of mortal terror and its mother was too frantic to care.

"Alas," cried the voice of Jean-Marie, "that they never told us what purgatory was like! What do the priests know? When we were threatened with punishment of our sins not a hint did we have of this. To sleep for a few hours, haunted with the moment of awakening! Then a cruel insult from the earth that is tired of us, and the orchestra of hell. Again! and again! and again! Oh God! How long? How long?"

The priest stumbled to his feet and ran over graves and paths to the mound above the countess. There he would hear a voice praising the monster of night and dawn, a note of content in this terrible chorus of despair which he believed would drive him mad. He vowed that on the morrow he would move his dead, if he had to un-bury them with his own hands and carry them up the hill to graves of his own making.

For a moment he heard no sound. He knelt and laid his ear to the grave, then pressed it more closely and held his breath. A long rumbling moan reached it, then another and another. But there were no words.

"Is she moaning in sympathy with my poor friends?" he thought; "or have they terrified her? Why does she not speak to them? Perhaps they would forget their plight were she to tell them of the world they have left so long. But it was not their world. Perhaps that it is which distresses her, for she will be lonelier here than on earth. Ah!"

A sharp horrified cry pierced to his ears, then a gasping shriek, and another; all dying away in a dreadful smothered rumble.

The priest rose and wrung his hands, looking to the wet skies for inspiration.

"Alas!" he sobbed, "she is not content. She has made a terrible mistake. She would rest in the deep sweet peace of death, and that monster of iron and fire and the frantic dead about her are tormenting a soul so tormented in life. There may be rest for her in the vault behind the castle, but not here. I know, and I shall do my duty—now, at once."

He gathered his robes about him and ran as fast as his old legs and rheumatic feet would take him towards the château, whose lights gleamed through the rain. On the bank of the river he met a fisherman and begged to be taken by boat. The fisherman wondered, but picked the priest up in his strong arms, lowered him into the boat, and rowed swiftly towards the château. When they landed he made fast.

"I will wait for you in the kitchen, my father," he said; and the priest blessed him and hurried up to the castle.

Once more he entered through the door of the great kitchen, with its blue tiles, its glittering brass and bronze warming-pans which had comforted nobles and monarchs in the days of Croisac splendor. He sank into a chair beside the stove while a maid hastened to the count. She returned while the priest was still shivering, and announced that her master would see his holy visitor in the library.

It was a dreary room where the count sat waiting for the priest, and it smelled of musty calf, for the books on the shelves were old. A few novels and newspapers lay on the heavy table, a fire burned on the andirons, but the paper on the wall was very dark and the fleurs-de-lis were tarnished and dull. The count, when at home, divided his time between this library and the water, when he could not chase the boar or the stag in the forests. But he often went to Paris, where he could afford the life of a bachelor in a wing of his great hotel; he had known too much of the extravagance of women to give his wife the key of the faded salons. He had loved the beautiful girl when he married her, but her repinings and bitter discontent had alienated him, and during the past year he had held himself aloof from her in sullen resentment. Too late he understood, and dreamed passionately of atonement. She had been a high-spirited, brilliant, eager creature, and her unsatisfied mind had dwelt constantly on the world she had vividly enjoyed for one year. And he had given her so little in return!

He rose as the priest entered, and bowed low. The visit bored him, but the good old priest commanded his respect; moreover, he had performed many offices and rites in his family. He moved a chair towards his guest, but the old man shook his head and nervously twisted his hands together.

"Alas, *Monsieur le Comte*," he said, "it may be that you, too, will tell me that I am an old lunatic, as did *Monsieur l'Évêque*. Yet I must speak, even if you tell your servants to fling me out of the château."

The count had started slightly. He

recalled certain acid comments of the bishop, followed by a statement that a young *curé* should be sent, gently to supersede the old priest, who was in his dotage. But he replied suavely:

"You know, my father, that no one in this castle will ever show you disrespect. Say what you wish; have no fear. But will you not sit down? I am very tired."

The priest took the chair and fixed his eyes appealingly on the count.

"It is this, Monsieur." He spoke rapidly, lest his courage should go. "That terrible train, with its brute of iron and live coals and foul smoke and screeching throat, has awakened my dead. I guarded them with holy water and they heard it not, until one night when I missed—I was with Madame as the train shrieked by shaking the nails out of the coffins. I hurried back, but the mischief was done, the dead were awake, the dear sleep of eternity was shattered. They thought it was

the last trump and wondered why they still were in their graves. But they talked together and it was not so bad at the first. But now they are frantic. They are in hell, and I have come to beseech you to see that they are moved far up on the hill. Ah, think, think, Monsieur, what it is to have the last long sleep of the grave so rudely disturbed—the sleep for which we live and endure so patiently!"

He stopped abruptly and caught his breath. The count had listened without change of countenance, convinced that he was facing a madman. But the farce wearied him, and involuntarily his hand had moved towards a bell on the table.

"Ah, Monsieur, not yet! not yet!" panted the priest. "It is of the countess I came to speak. I had forgotten. She told me she wished to lie there and listen to the train go by to Paris, so I sprinkled no holy water on her grave. But she, too, is wretched and horror-stricken, Monsieur. She moans and screams. Her coffin is new and strong, and I cannot hear her words, but I have heard those frightful sounds from her grave tonight, Monsieur; I swear it on the cross. Ah, Monsieur, thou dost believe me at last!"

For the count, as white as the woman had been in her coffin, and shaking from head to foot, had staggered from his chair and was staring at the priest as if he saw the ghost of his countess.

"You heard—?" he gasped.

"She is not at peace, Monsieur. She moans and shrieks in a terrible, smothered way, as if a hand were on her mouth—"

But he had uttered the last of his words. The count had suddenly recovered himself and dashed from the room. The priest passed his hand across his forehead and sank slowly to the floor.

"He will see that I spoke the truth," he thought, as he fell asleep, "and tomorrow he will intercede for my poor friends."

THE PRIEST LIES HIGH ON the hill where no train will ever disturb him, and his old comrades of the violated cemetery are close about him. For the Count and Countess of Croisac, who adore his memory, hastened to give him in death what he most had desired in the last of his life. And with them all things are well, for a man, too, may be born again, and without descending into the grave.

 ertrude atherton (1857–1948) was an American novelist and short story writer.

eth's comics and drawings have appeared in the *New York Times*, the *New Yorker*, the *Globe and Mail*, and countless other publications.

His latest graphic novel, *Clyde Fans*, won the prestigious Festival d'Angoulême's Prix Spécial du Jury.

He lives in Guelph, Ontario, with his wife, Tania, in an old house he has named "Inkwell's End."

Publisher's note: "The Dead and the Countess" was first
published in 1905 by Harper & Brothers in *The Bell
in the Fog And Other Stories.*

Library and Archives Canada Cataloguing in Publication

Title: The dead and the countess : a ghost story for Christmas /
  Gertrude Atherton ; designed & decorated by Seth.
Names: Atherton, Gertrude Franklin Horn, 1857-1948, author.
  Seth, 1962- illustrator.
Description: Series statement: Seth's Christmas ghost stories
  Identifiers: Canadiana 20220261261
  ISBN 9781771965071 (softcover)
Subjects: LCGFT: Ghost stories. | LCGFT: Christmas fiction.
  | LCGFT: Short stories.
  Classification: LCC PS1042 .D43 2022
  DDC 813/.52—dc23

Readied for the press by Daniel Wells
Illustrated and designed by Seth
Copyedited by Ashley Van Elswyk
Typeset by Vanessa Stauffer

PRINTED AND BOUND IN CANADA